D1153054

WITHDRAWN

Published by Collins Educational
An imprint of HarperCollins*Publishers* Ltd
77-85 Fulham Palace Road
London W6 8JB

The HarperCollins website address is:
www.**fire**and**water**.com

© The Templar Company plc 1985
Letterland© was devised by and is the copyright of Lyn Wendon.

First published by Hamlyn Publishing 1985
Second edition published by Thomas Nelson and Sons Ltd 1989
This edition published 1996 by Collins Educational
Reprinted 1999, 2000

ISBN 0 00 303255 8

LETTERLAND® is a registered trademark of Lyn Wendon.

The author asserts the moral right to be identified
as the author of this work.

British Library Cataloguing in Publication Data
A catalogue record for this book is available from the British Library.

Printed by Printing Express Ltd, Hong Kong

LETTERLAND HOME LEARNING
HarperCollins publishes a wide range of Letterland early
learning books, video and audio tapes, puzzles and games.
For an information leaflet about Letterland or to order materials
call 0870 0100 441.

The Hairy Hat Man's House

Written by Lyn Wendon
Illustrated by Jane Launchbury

Collins

An imprint of HarperCollins*Publishers*

Harry was a little boy who loved hats. Little hats, big hats, tall hats and short hats. Anything he could put on his head made him happy. As he grew older, collecting hats became his hobby. Soon he had nearly a hundred hats.

When Harry became a man, he still loved hats. So one day he started a hat shop in the little house where he lived, half way up a hill.

L ots of people came to buy hats from his hat shop.
They could buy any hat they wanted, except one. That was because one of Harry's hats was not for sale.

It was his favourite hat – a green, rather hairy hat. He had made it himself and he wore it all the time.

Soon people stopped calling him Harry. They always called him the 'Hairy Hat Man' instead.

The Hairy Hat Man lived happily in his little house, until one evening there was a great storm in Letterland.
The wind blew hard and the rain poured down. The storm was still raging when he went to bed.
When he woke up the next morning the poor Hat Man had a terrible shock.

"Heavens!" he cried. "The wind has blown a hole in my roof.
Now all my hats are soaked!"

He carried the dripping hats outside and hung them on the line to dry.
He felt very unhappy.

"Henry," he said to his horse, "where will I get the money to buy a new roof?"

"You'll just have to sell lots more hats," said Henry.

"But how?" asked the Hairy Hat Man. "It is a long walk up the hill to my hat shop. I can't make the hill any shorter, can I?"

"You could take the hats down the hill and sell them in the market!" said Henry.

"But how will I ever carry them all?" asked the Hairy Hat Man.
"By horse?" suggested Henry, smiling.
"What a good idea!" cried Harry.

As soon as his hats were dry, the Hairy Hat Man harnessed Henry to a cart and loaded it high with hats. Together they set off down the hill.

In the market place it was very busy. The Hairy Hat Man stopped the cart to give Henry some hay.

Soon lots of the people had gathered round to buy hats. It was hot work, but the Hat Man and Henry hoped to sell enough hats to pay for a new roof before it rained again.

Every day they worked in the market place. They sold so many hats that soon the people had all the hats they needed ... but the Hat Man STILL did not have enough money for a new roof.

"It's hopeless," he said to his horse. "I don't know what to do now, Henry."

Henry's ears twitched as he tried to think.
"I can't think in this hot sun," he said. "Please make me a sun hat!"

"What a good idea!" said Harry. So straight away he made a large sun hat for Henry, with two holes in just the right places for his ears.

Soon all the other horses in Letterland heard about Henry's hat. They wanted to buy sun hats, too.

The next day, Bouncy Ben came along and asked, "Can you make me a special baseball cap?"

"I'd be happy to," said the Hairy Hat Man. So he made a special baseball cap for Bouncy Ben, with two holes in just the right places for his ears.

When Bouncy Ben's brothers saw his baseball cap, they all wanted one just like it. So the Hat Man made special caps for them too.

The next day, Clever Cat came along. She liked Henry's hat very much. "Can you make me a special cat hat?" she asked.

"Of course," said the Hat Man. So he made a special cat hat for her, with two holes in just the right places for her ears.

When Clever Cat's cousins saw her special hat they all wanted to buy one too. So Harry made lots more.

Soon the Hairy Hat Man had made a special hat for almost every animal in Letterland. But he STILL did not have enough money for the new roof.

"Henry," he said to his horse one day. "There is still only enough money for half a roof. We'll never have enough before it rains again. NOW what shall we do?"

Henry's ears twitched in their hat holes as he thought. Then he had an idea.

"If you can make sun hats for heads," he said, "why can't you make a rain hat for your house?"

"Of course!" cried the Hairy Hat Man, hopping up and down with excitement. "I could make a huge rain hat! If I make it myself it won't cost very much at all!"

That very same day he started
to make a special hat for his
house. It was huge, and it had
two holes in just the right places for
his chimneys.

When it was finished, his Letterland
friends helped to put the new hat on
his house.

At last the Hairy Hat Man was happy again. Now it didn't matter if it rained … his house had a new roof!

"Everyone likes my new roof, don't they, Henry!" he said to his horse.

Henry smiled. "That's because it looks like your favourite hat," said Henry.

The Hairy Hat Man looked at his new roof again. "It does rather, doesn't it," he said, smiling happily.

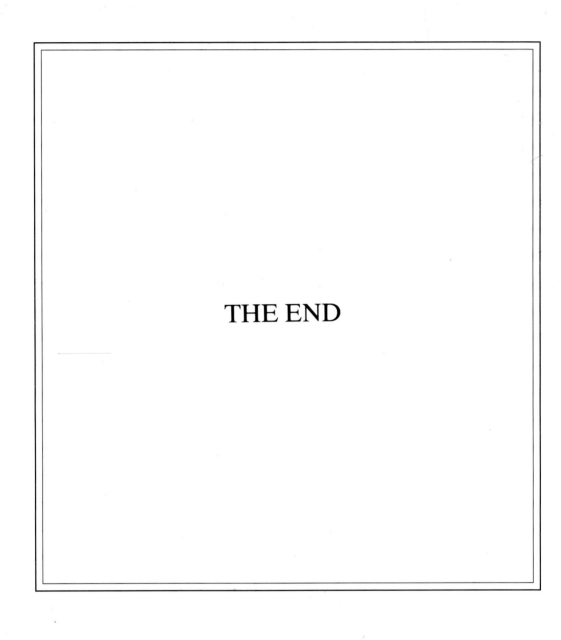

THE END